For Frances ~ P H

For my two little superheroes,
Dara and Walter ~ A W

LITTLE TIGER PRESS LTD,
an imprint of the Little Tiger Group
1 Coda Studios,
189 Munster Road,
London SW6 6AW
www.littletiger.co.uk

First published in Great Britain 2020

Text by Patricia Hegarty
Text copyright © Little Tiger Press Ltd 2020
Illustrations copyright © Alex Willmore 2020
Alex Willmore has asserted his right to
be identified as the illustrator of this work
under the Copyright, Designs and Patents Act, 1988
A CIP catalogue record for this book is available
from the British Library

Printed in China • LTP/1400/2943/0220

2 4 6 8 10 9 7 5 3 1

SUPERHERO BABY!

Patricia Hegarty

Alex Willmore

LITTLE TIGER

LONDON

Something strange is happening
as the clock strikes half past one –
Everybody's fast asleep,
well, almost everyone . . .

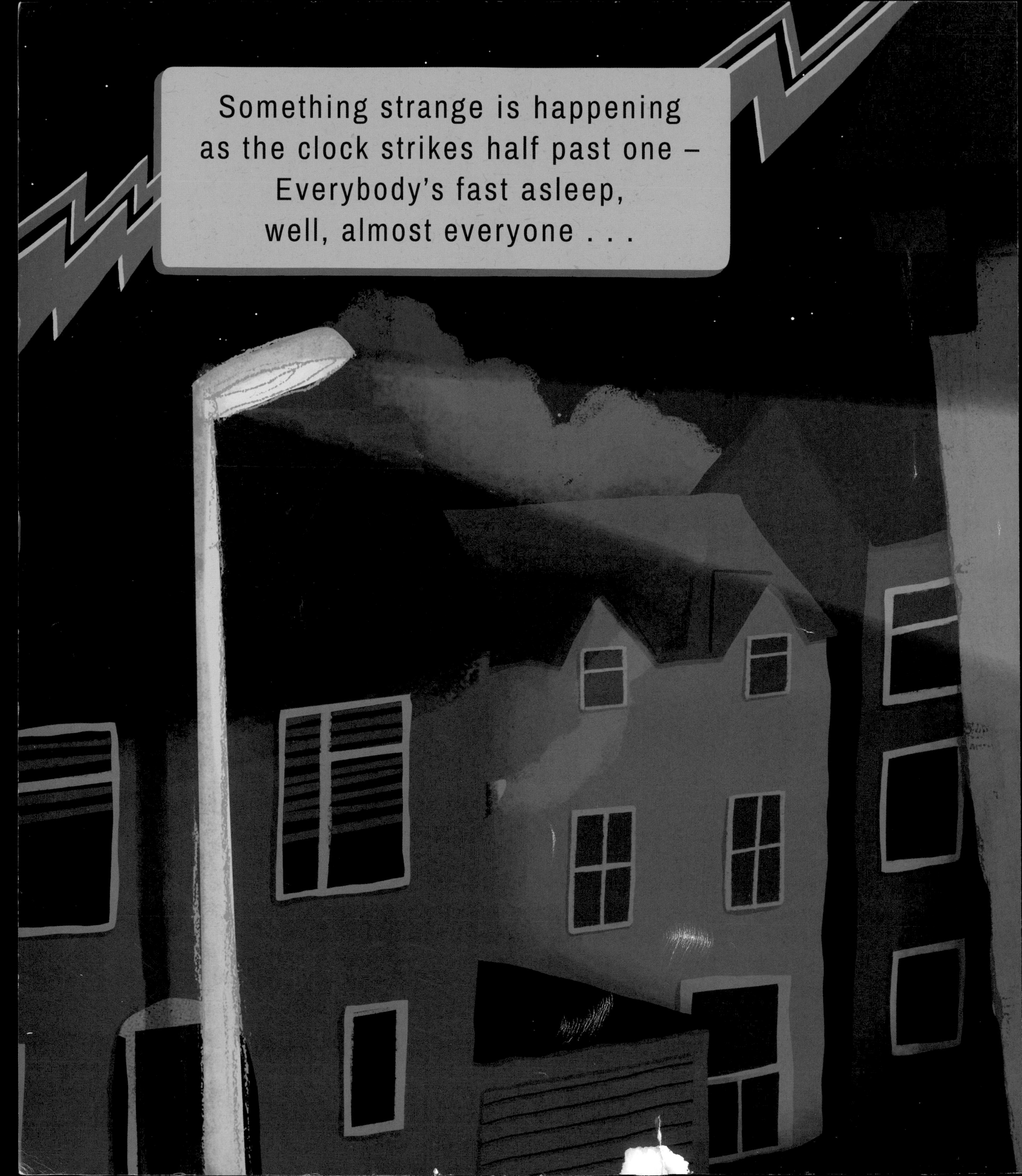

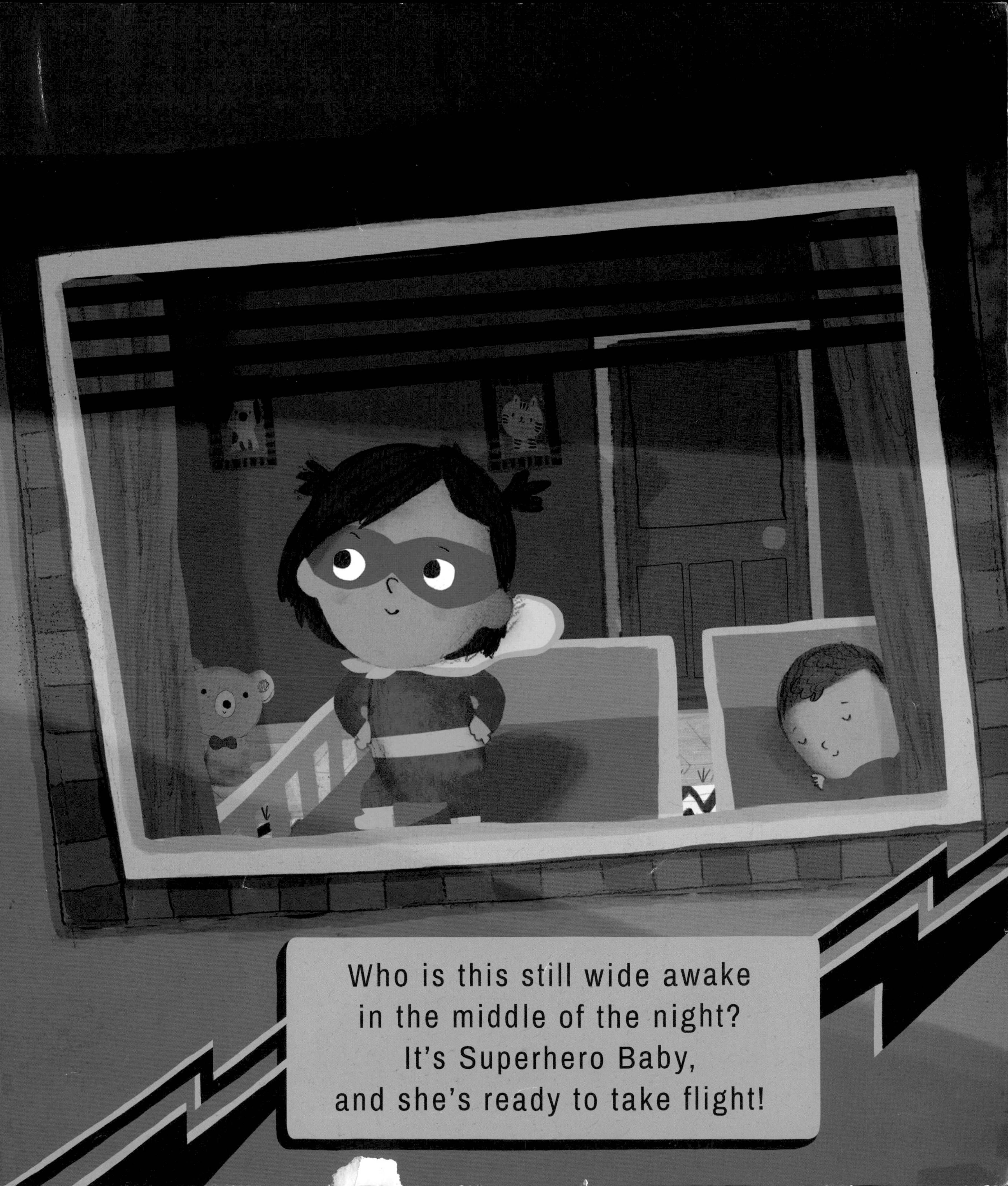

Who is this still wide awake
in the middle of the night?
It's Superhero Baby,
and she's ready to take flight!

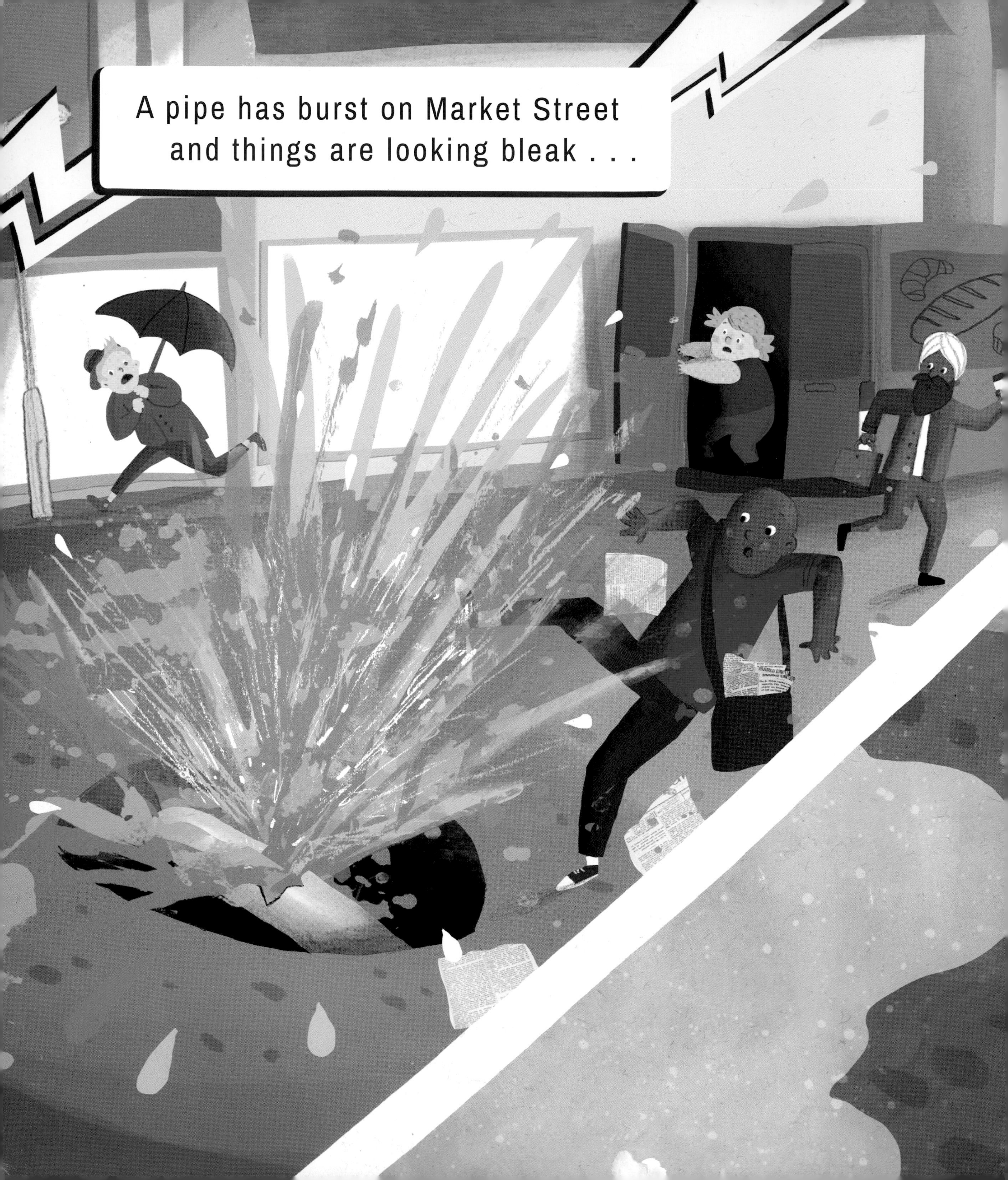
A pipe has burst on Market Street
and things are looking bleak . . .

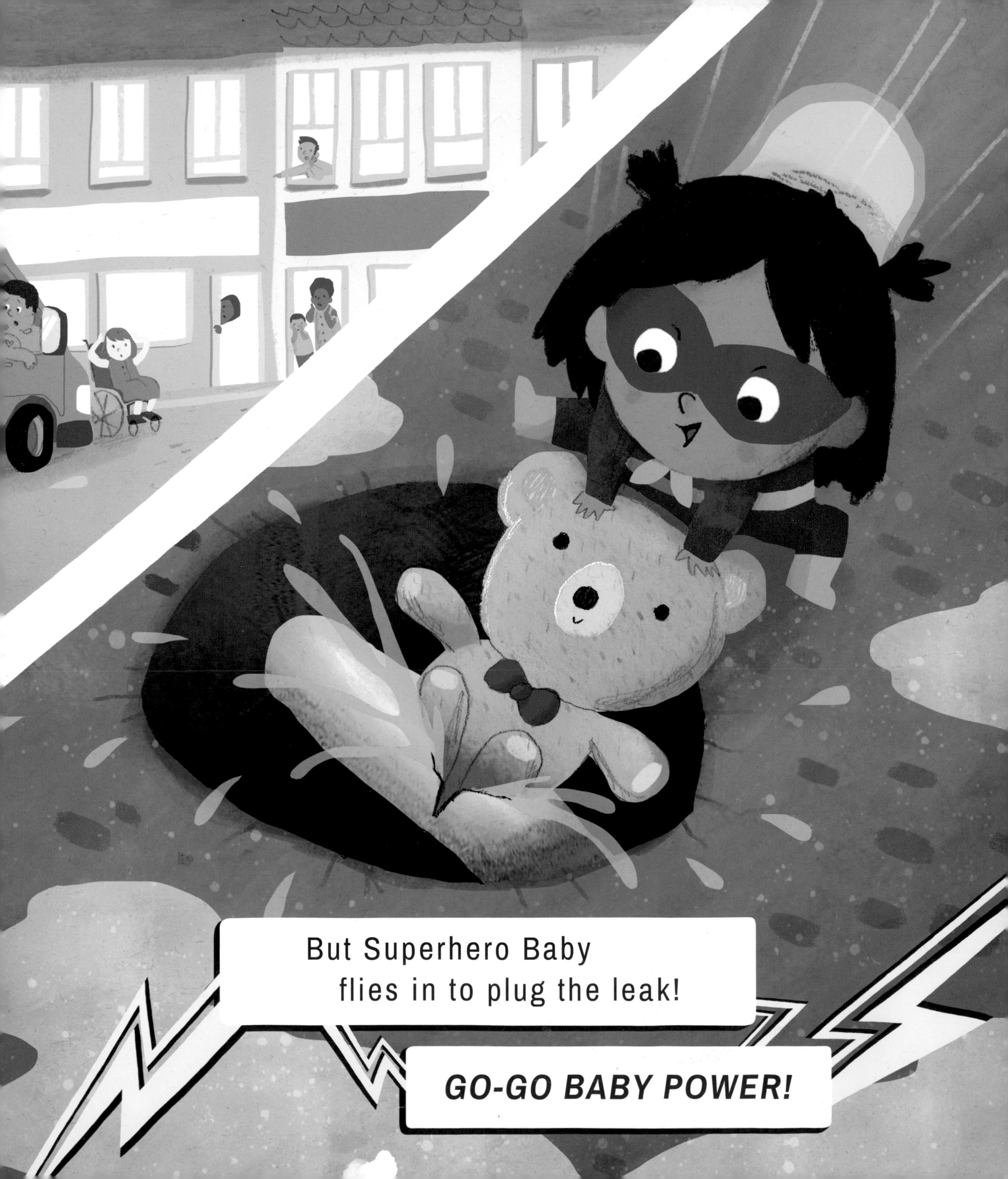

But Superhero Baby
flies in to plug the leak!

GO-GO BABY POWER!

Safely back inside her cot,
another day is dawning.

And Baby gurgles peacefully
when Mummy says . . .

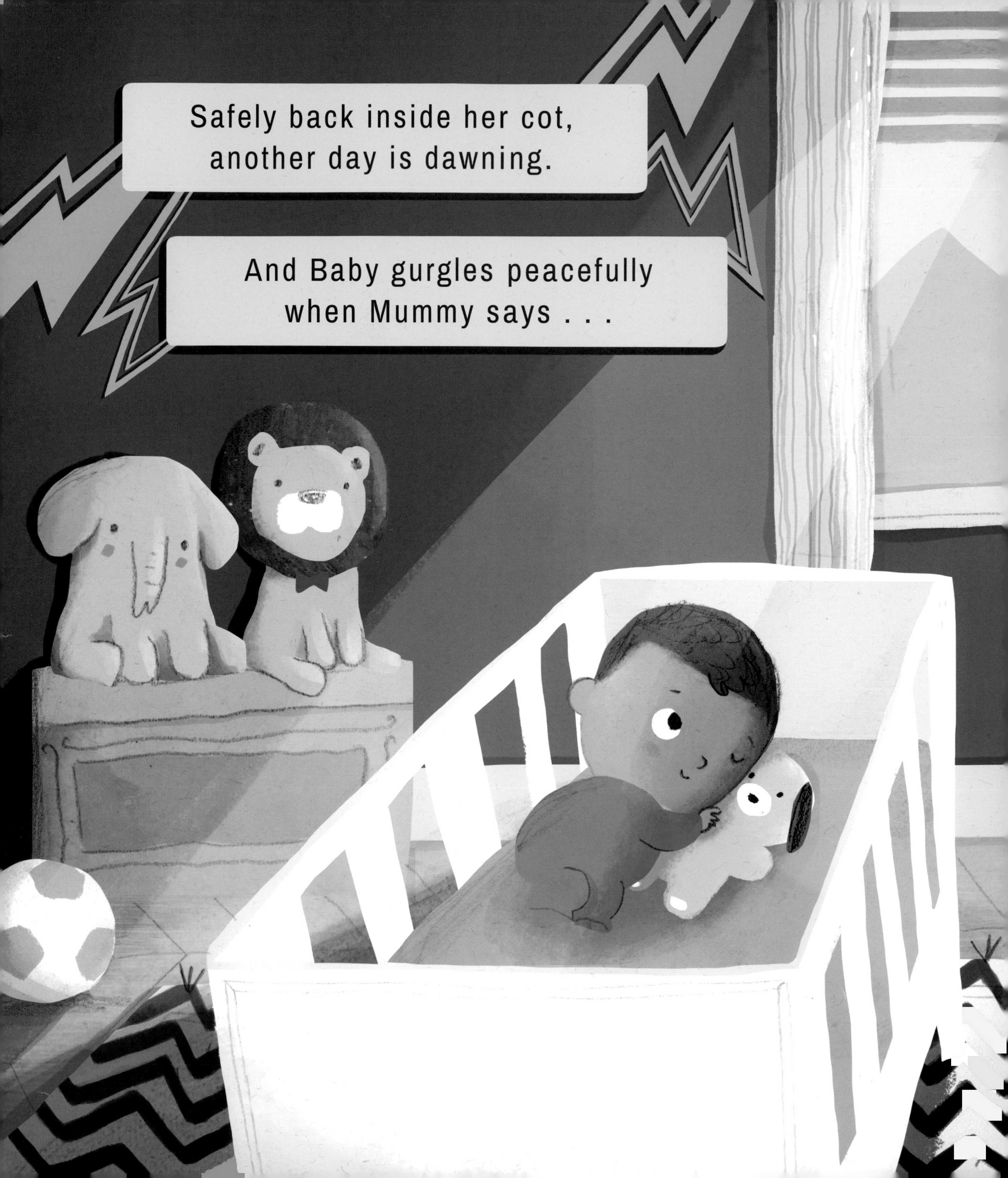

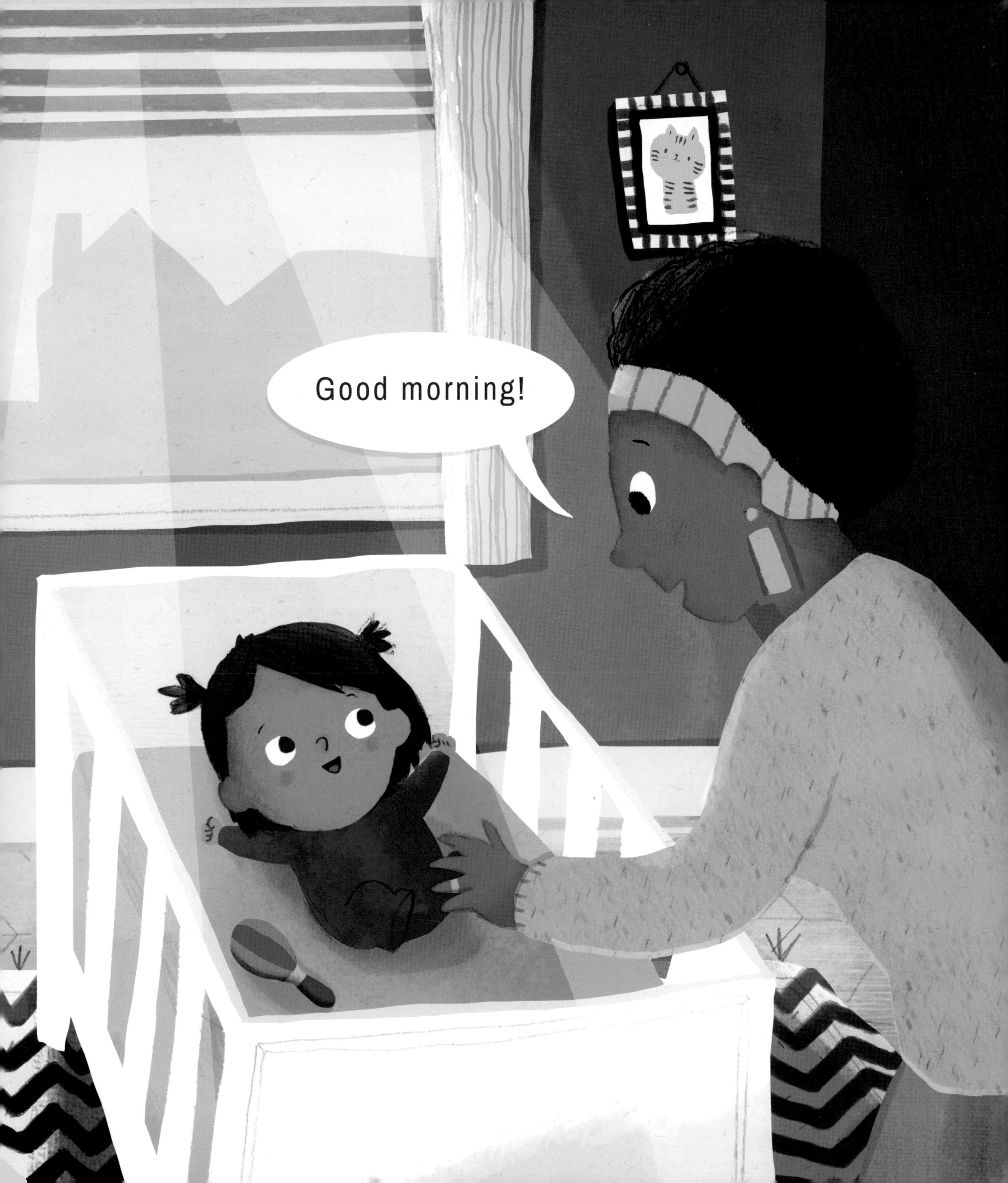
Good morning!

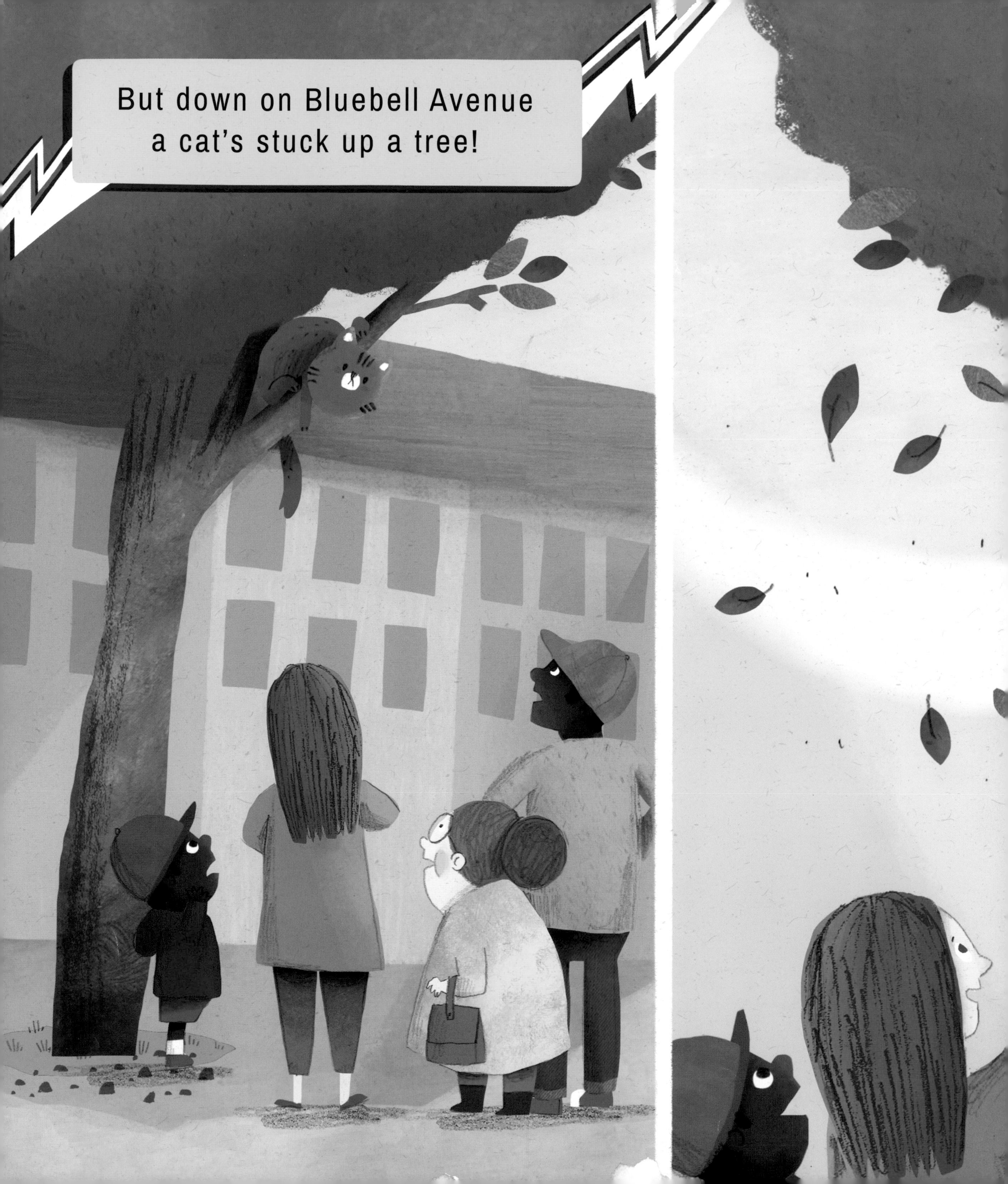
But down on Bluebell Avenue
a cat's stuck up a tree!

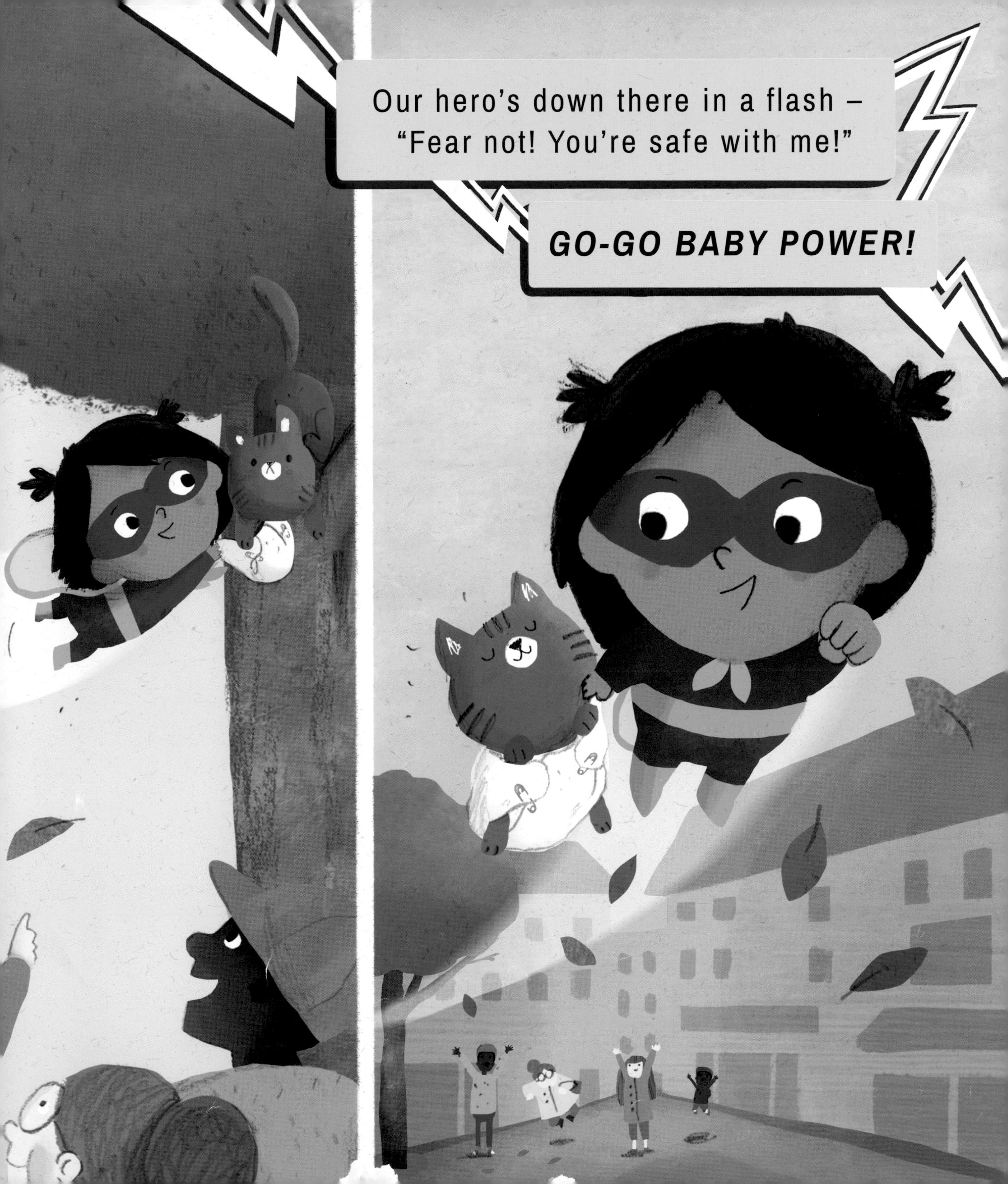
Our hero's down there in a flash –
"Fear not! You're safe with me!"
GO-GO BABY POWER!

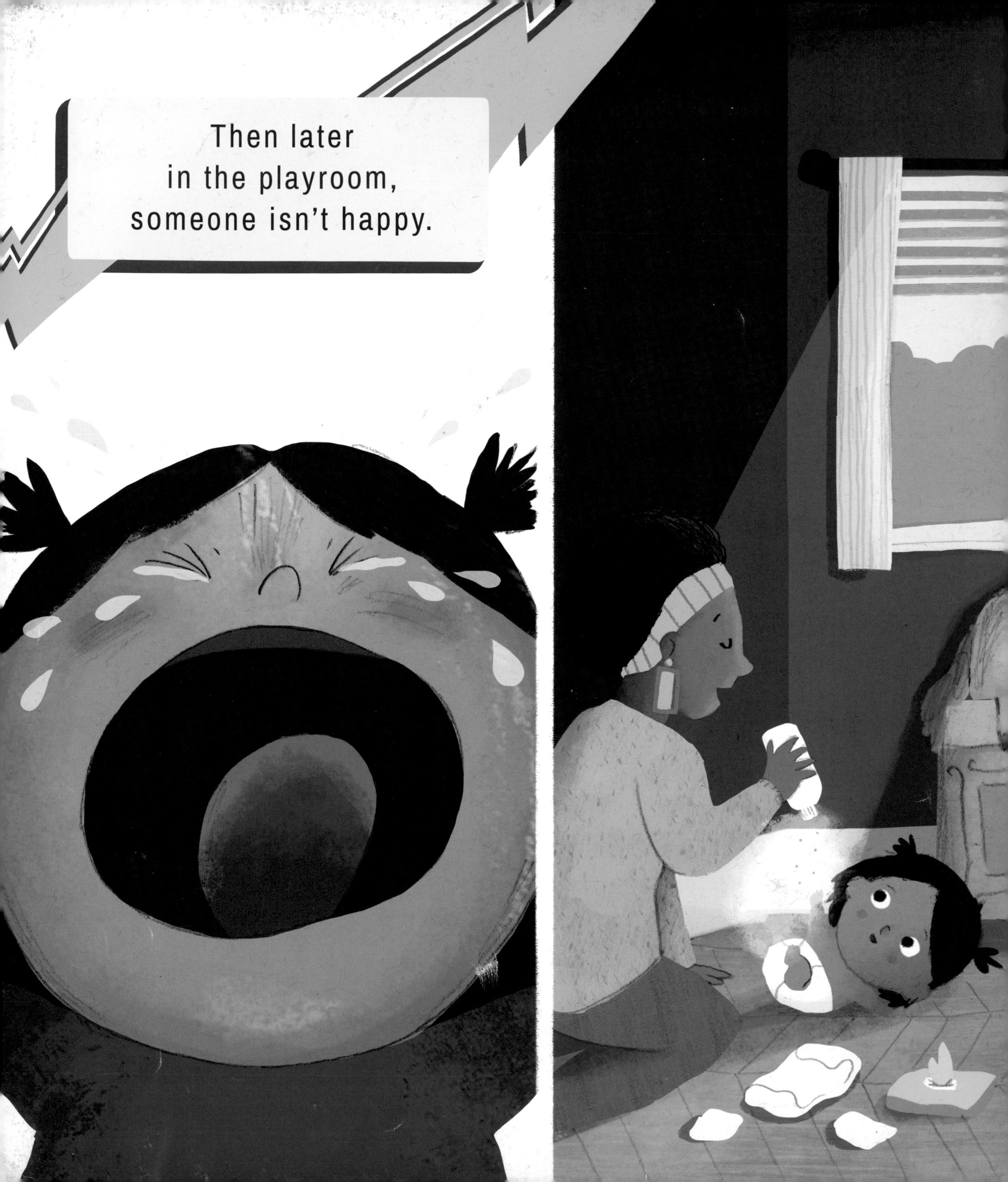
Then later in the playroom, someone isn't happy.

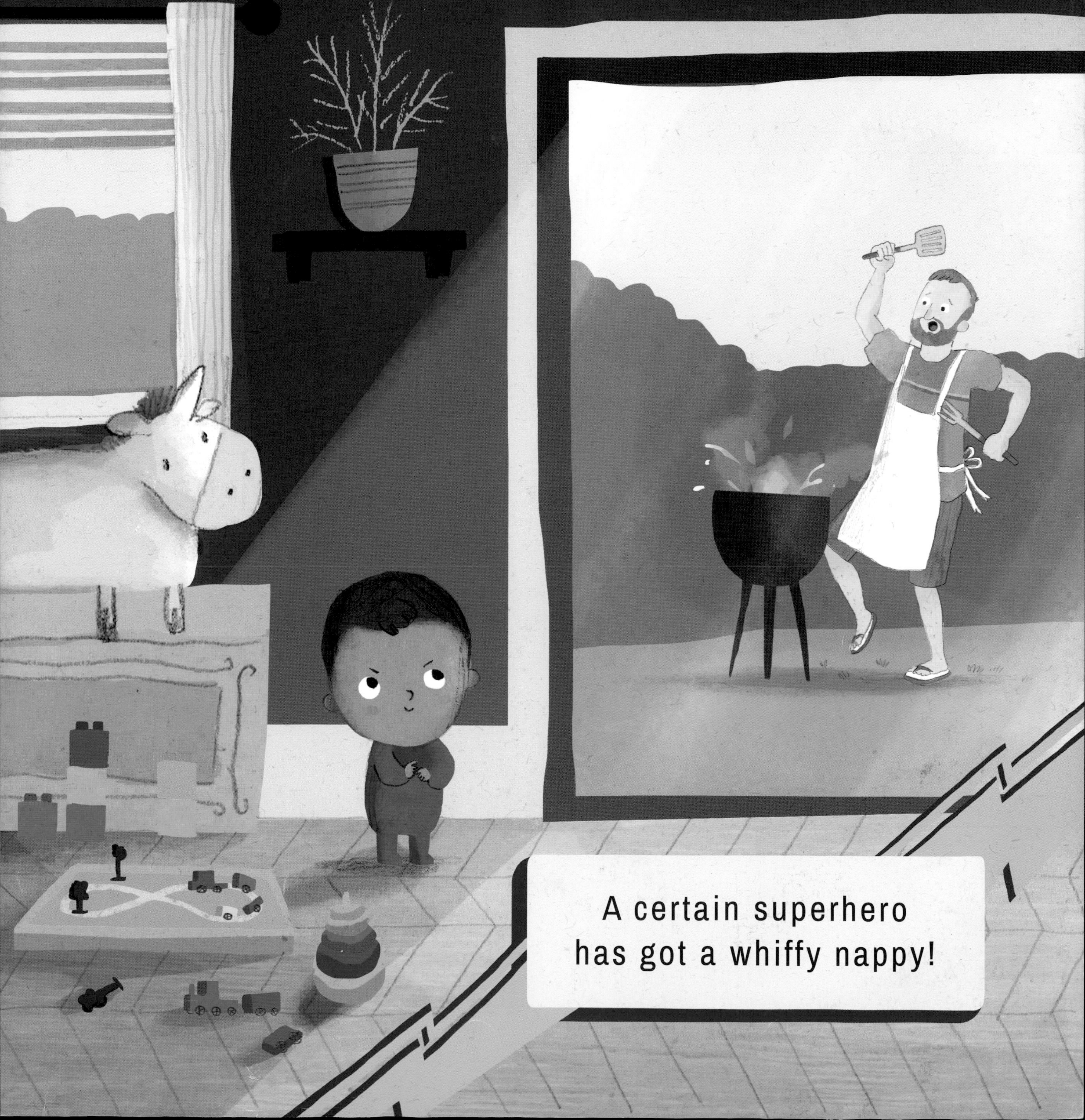

A certain superhero
has got a whiffy nappy!

"Help! The barbecue's caught fire!"

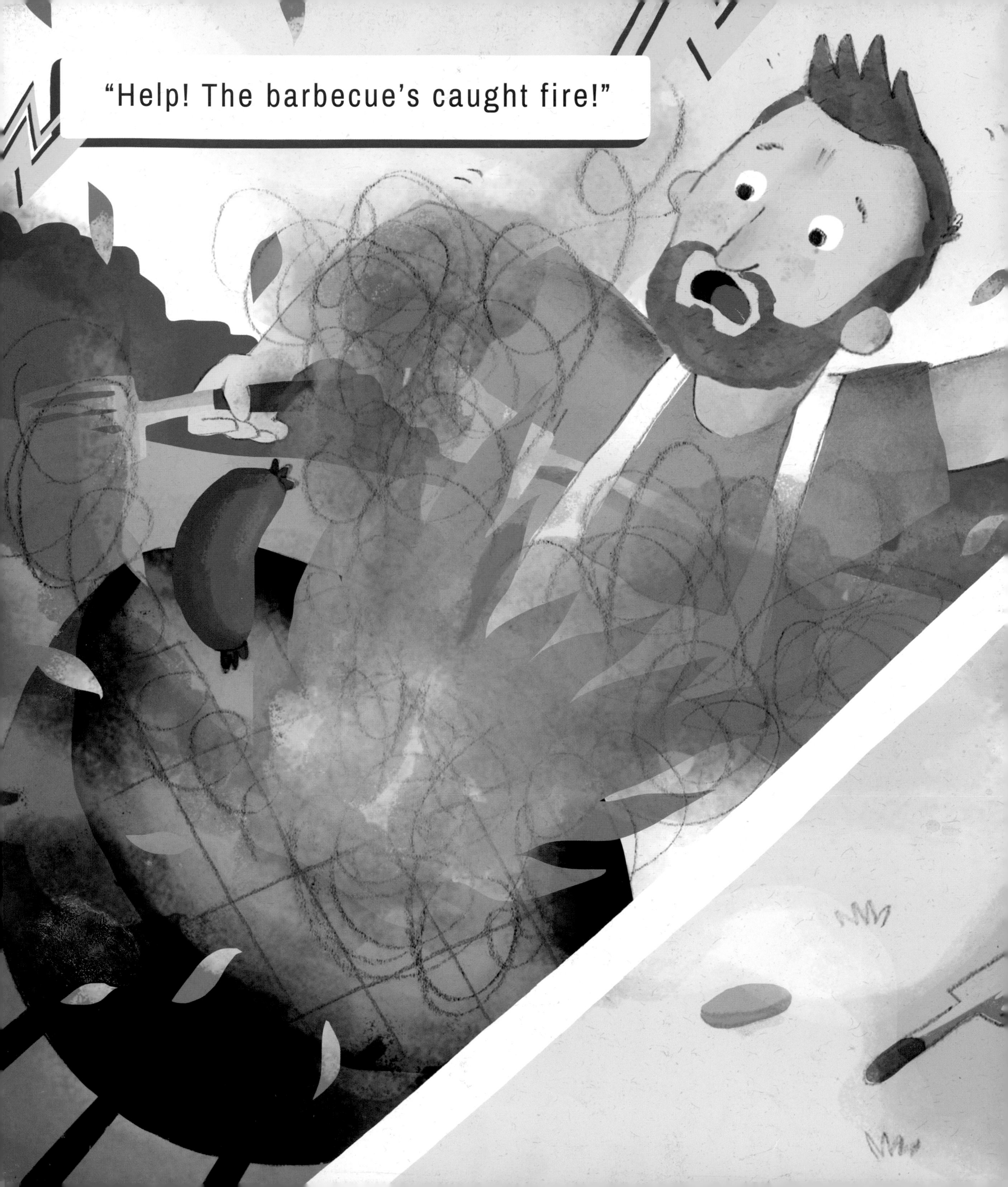

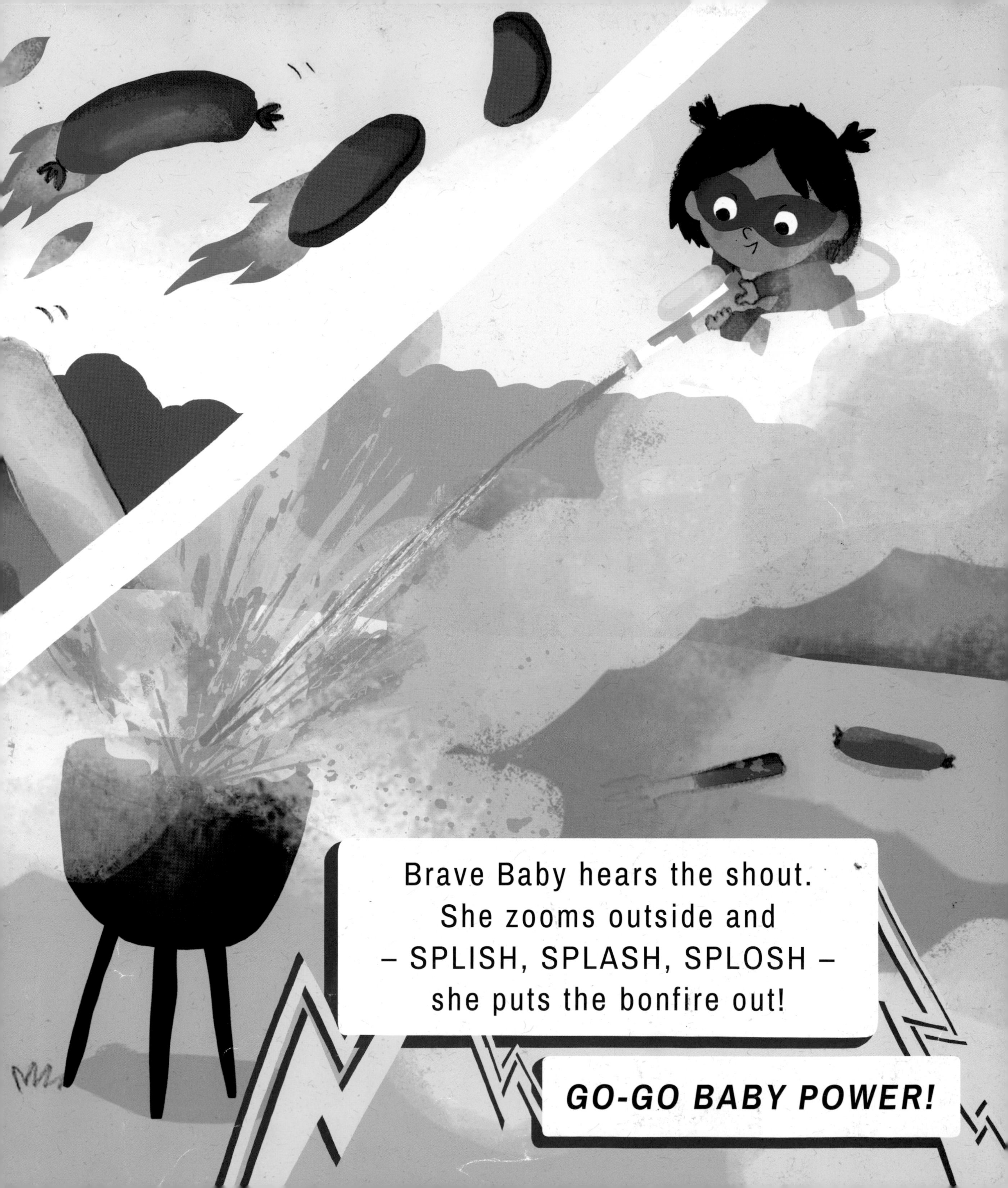

Brave Baby hears the shout.
She zooms outside and
– SPLISH, SPLASH, SPLOSH –
she puts the bonfire out!

GO-GO BABY POWER!

It’s time for Baby’s nap now,
but heroes never sleep!
(Unlike her perfect brother
who doesn’t make a peep.)

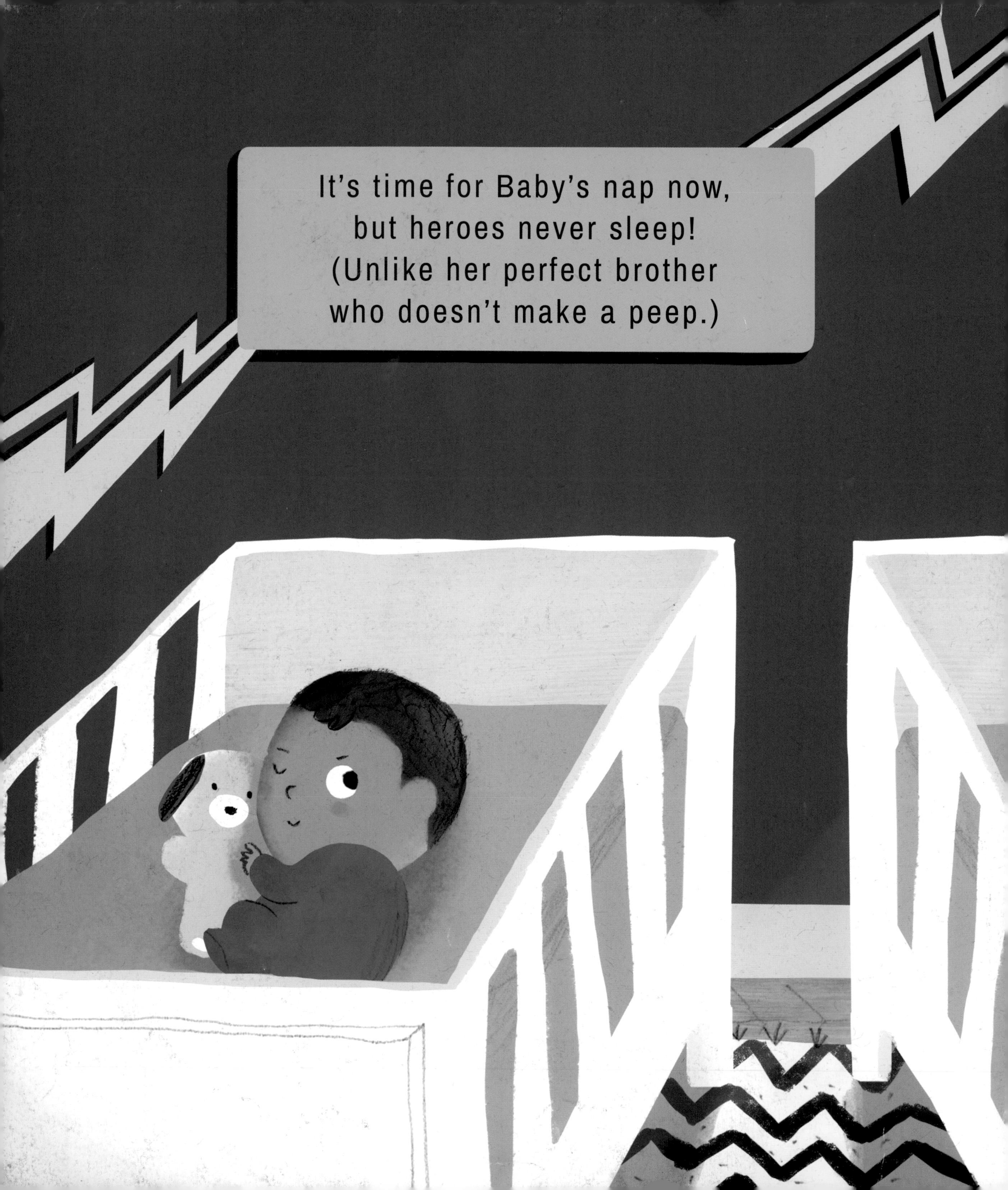

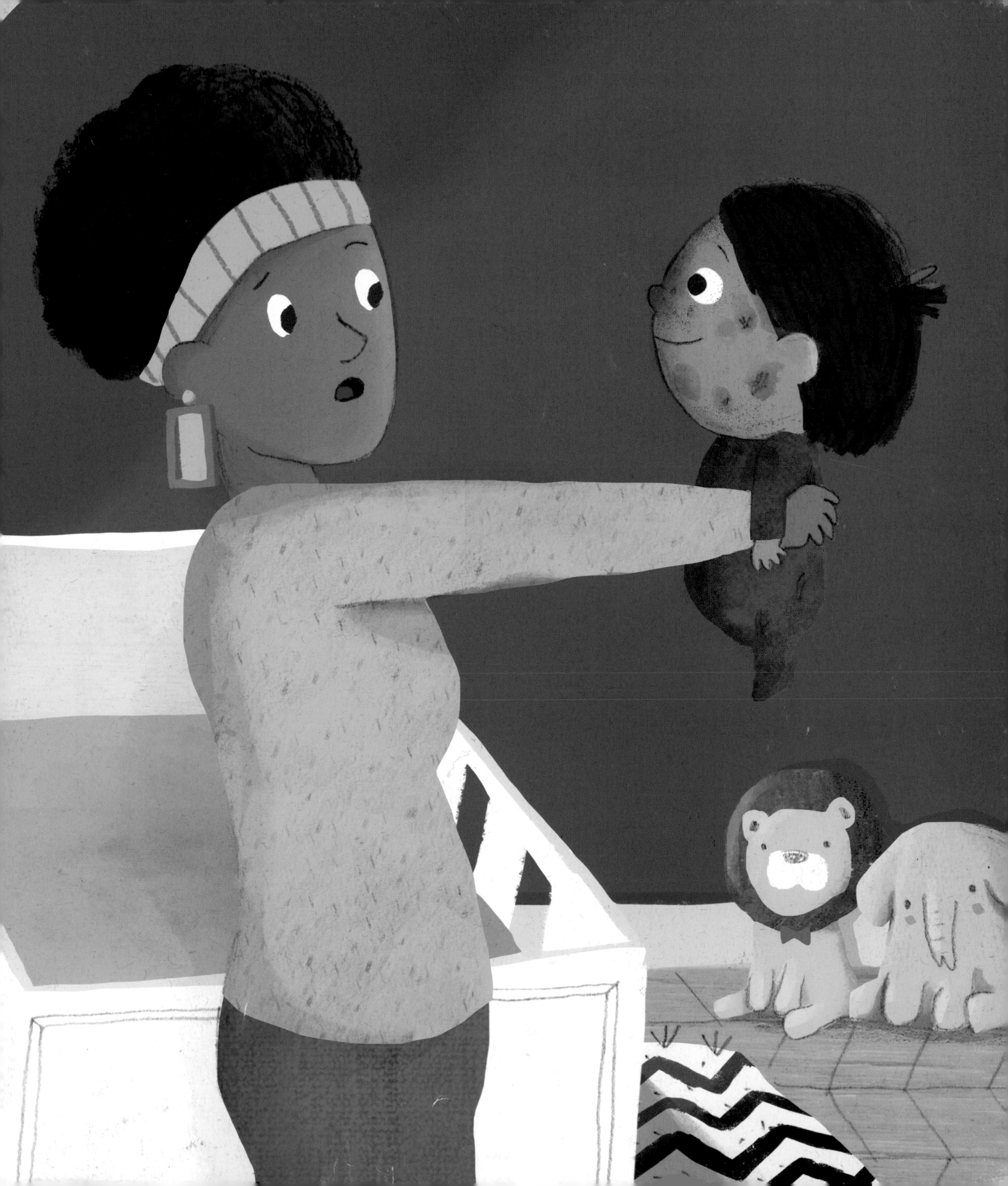

Poor Fido's in a pickle,
how can that dog escape?

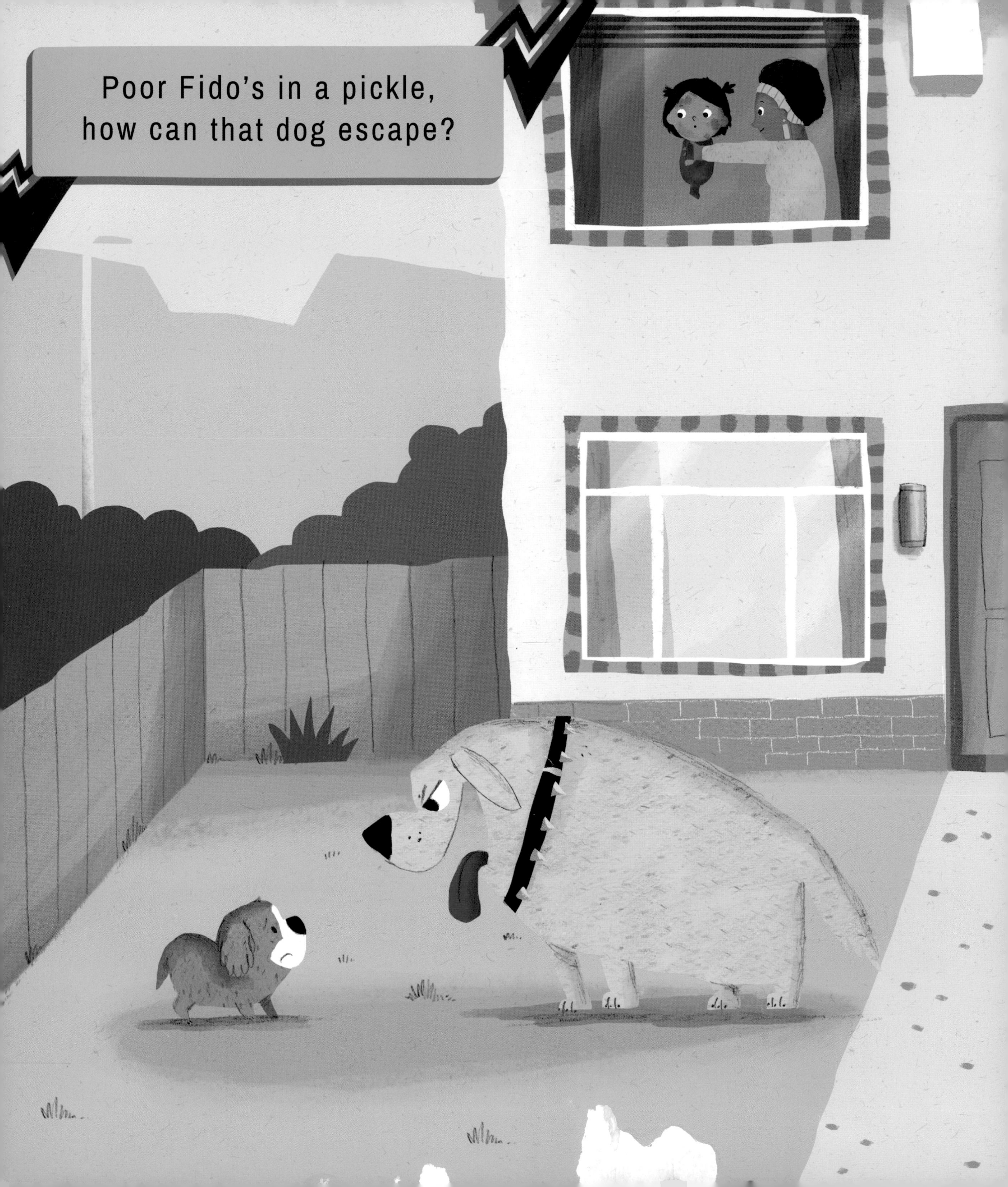

But look who's come to save him,
in her superhero cape!

GO-GO BABY POWER!

For Superhero Baby,
there's never time to rest.

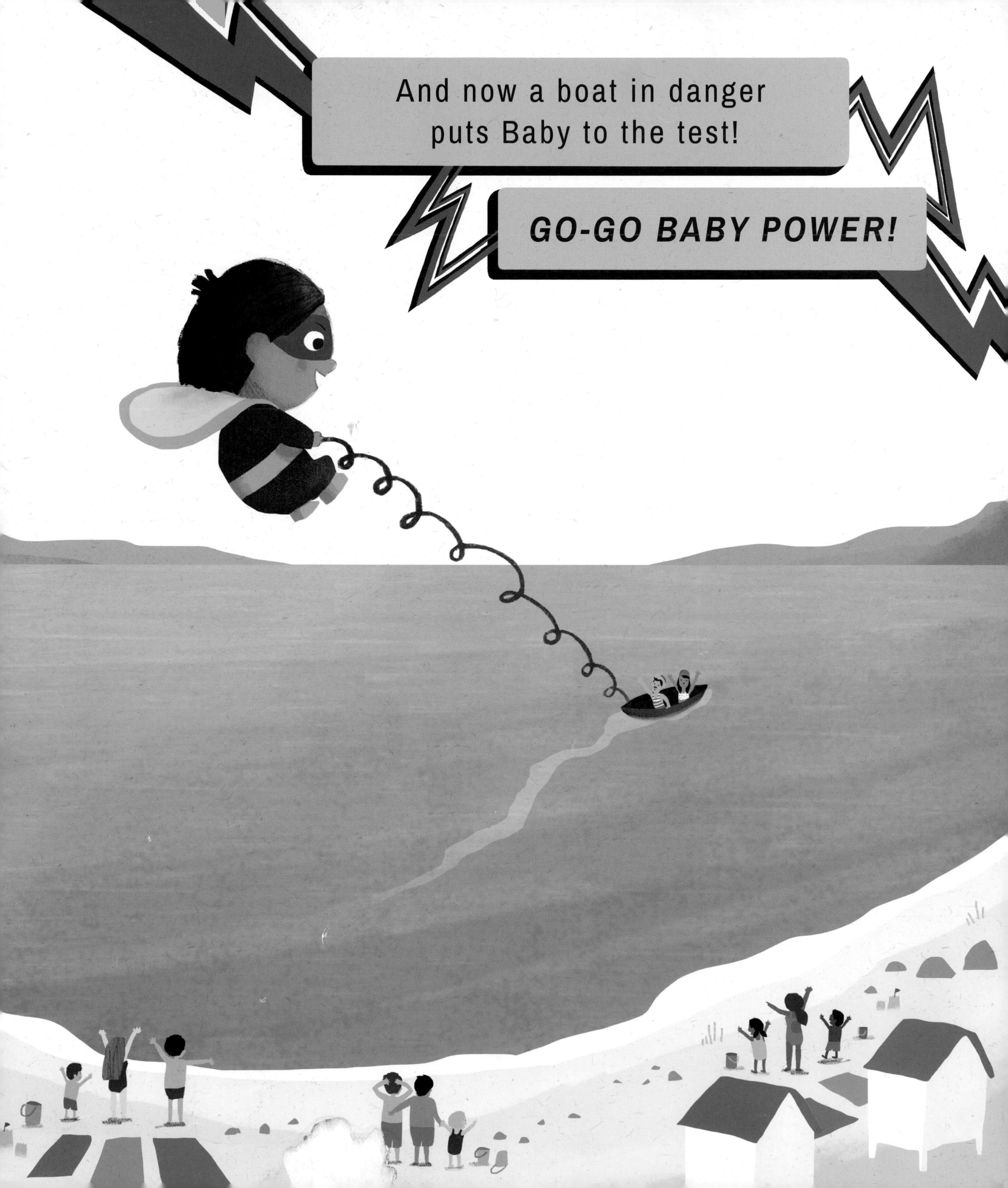
And now a boat in danger
puts Baby to the test!
GO-GO BABY POWER!

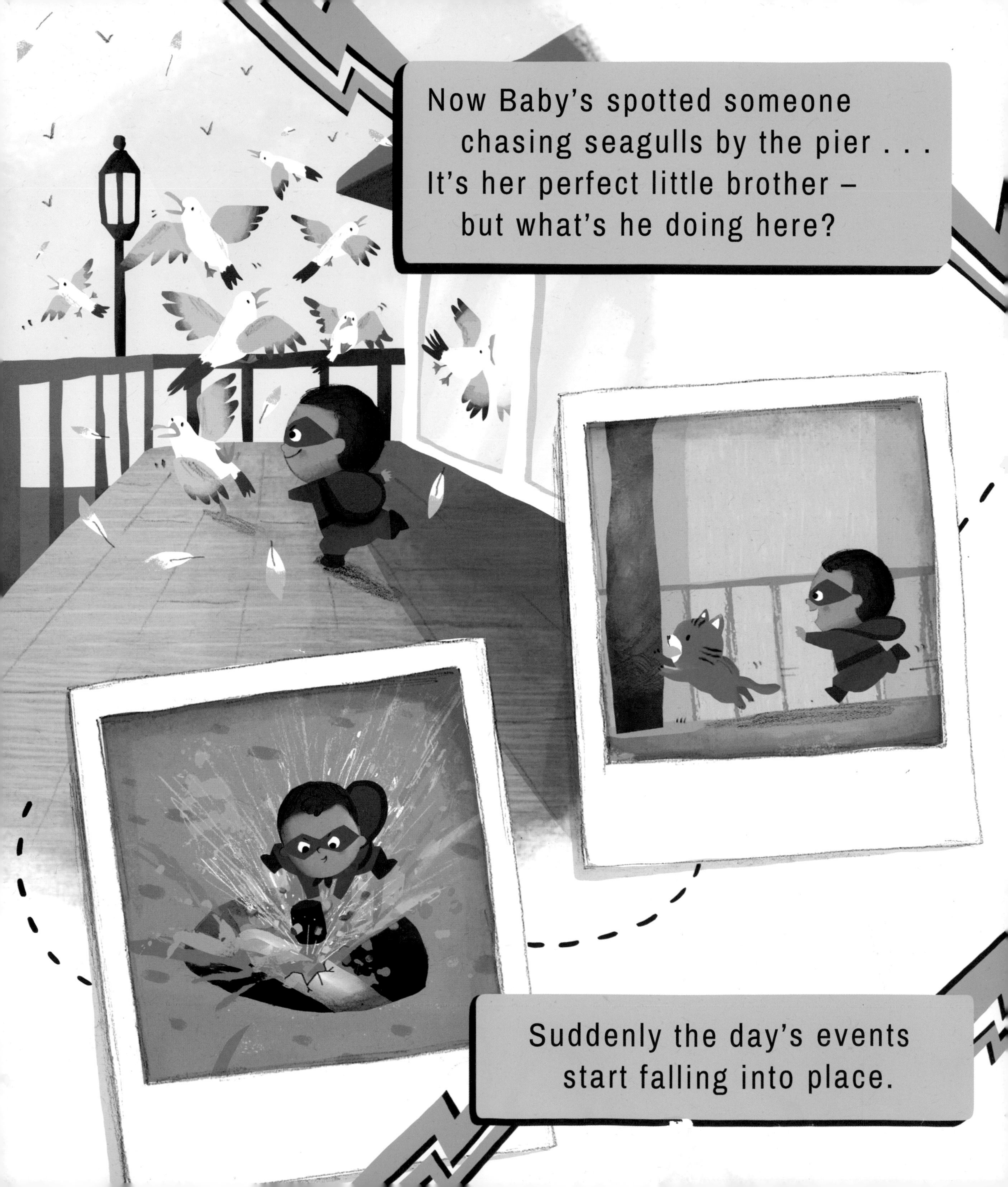

Now Baby's spotted someone
chasing seagulls by the pier . . .
It's her perfect little brother –
but what's he doing here?

Suddenly the day's events
start falling into place.

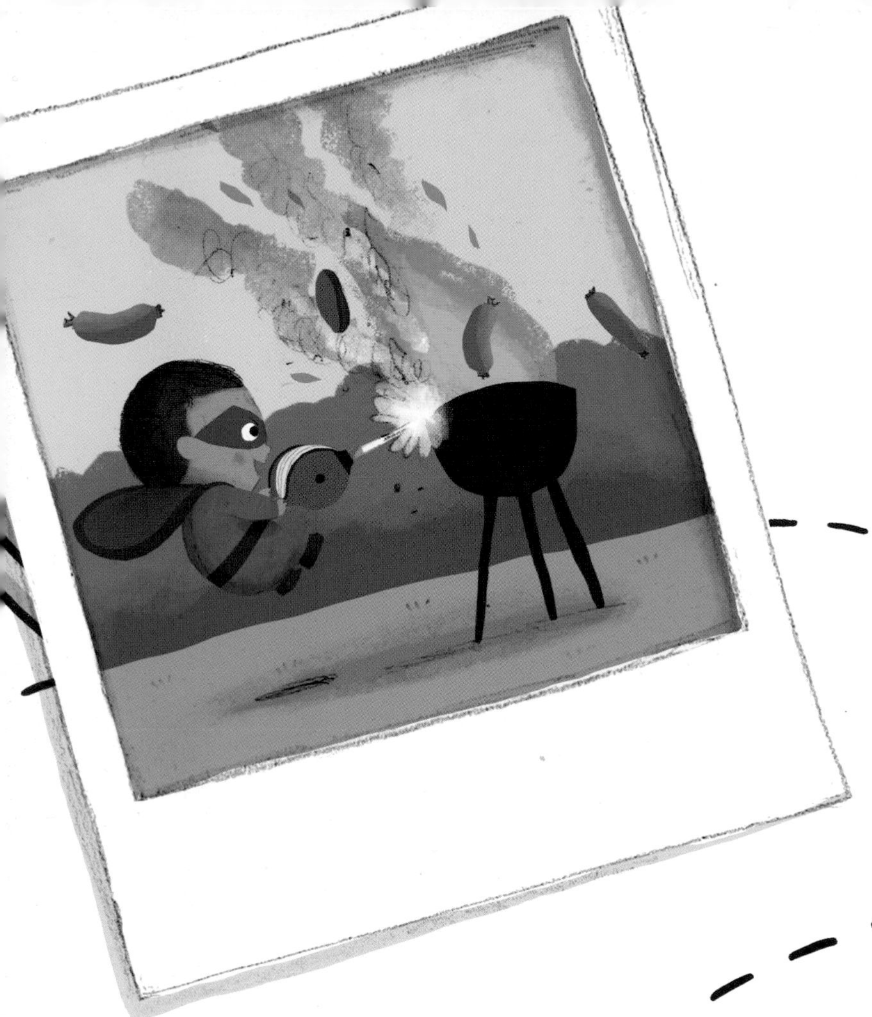

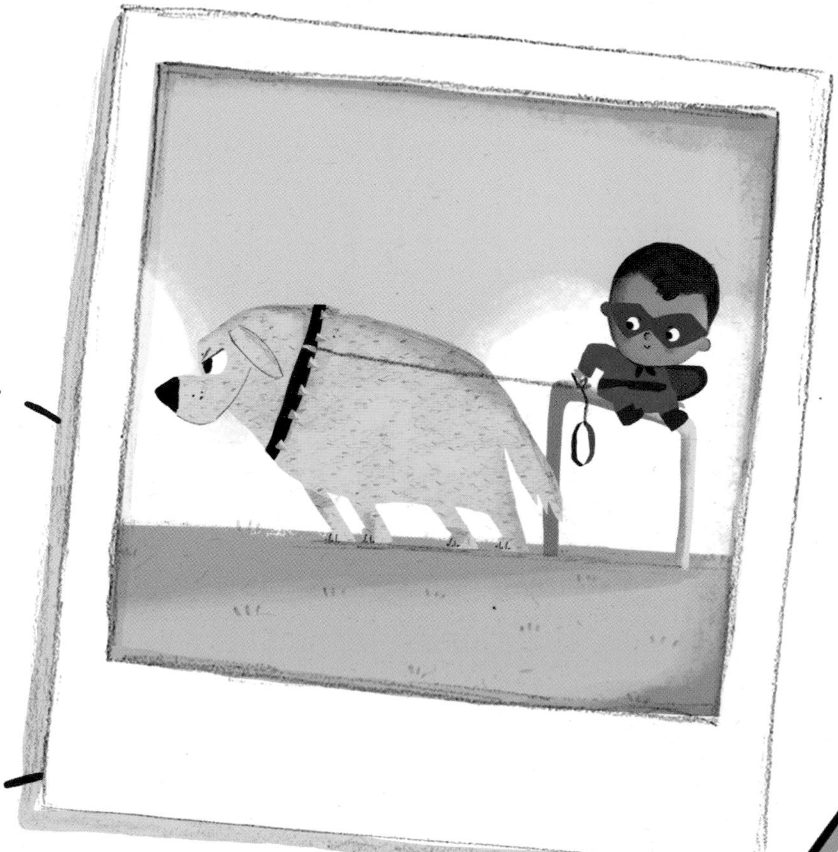

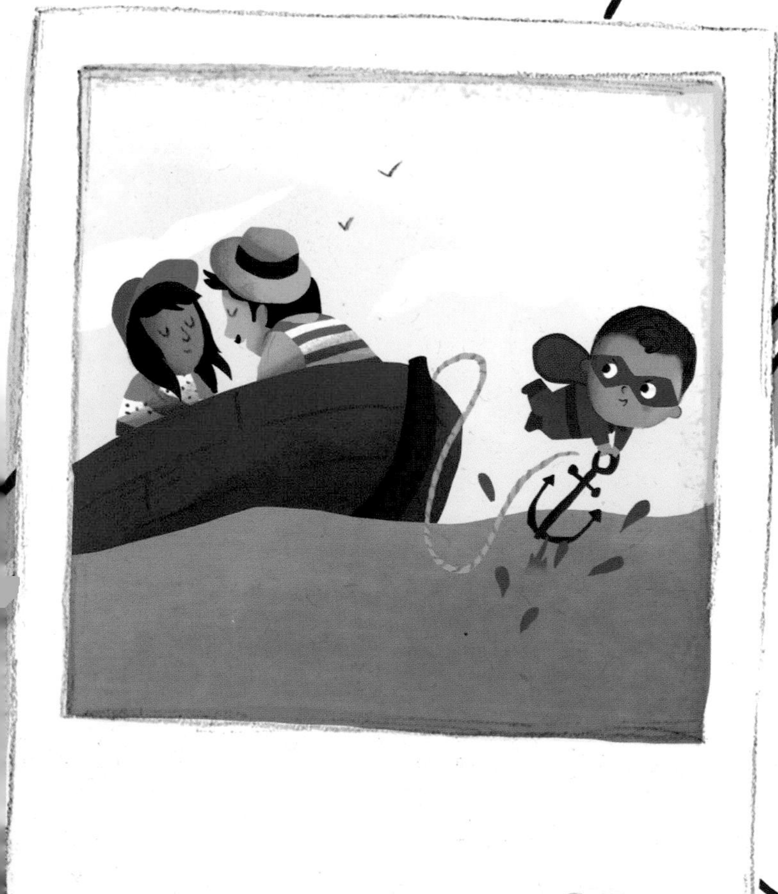

Brave Baby and her nemesis are standing face to face.

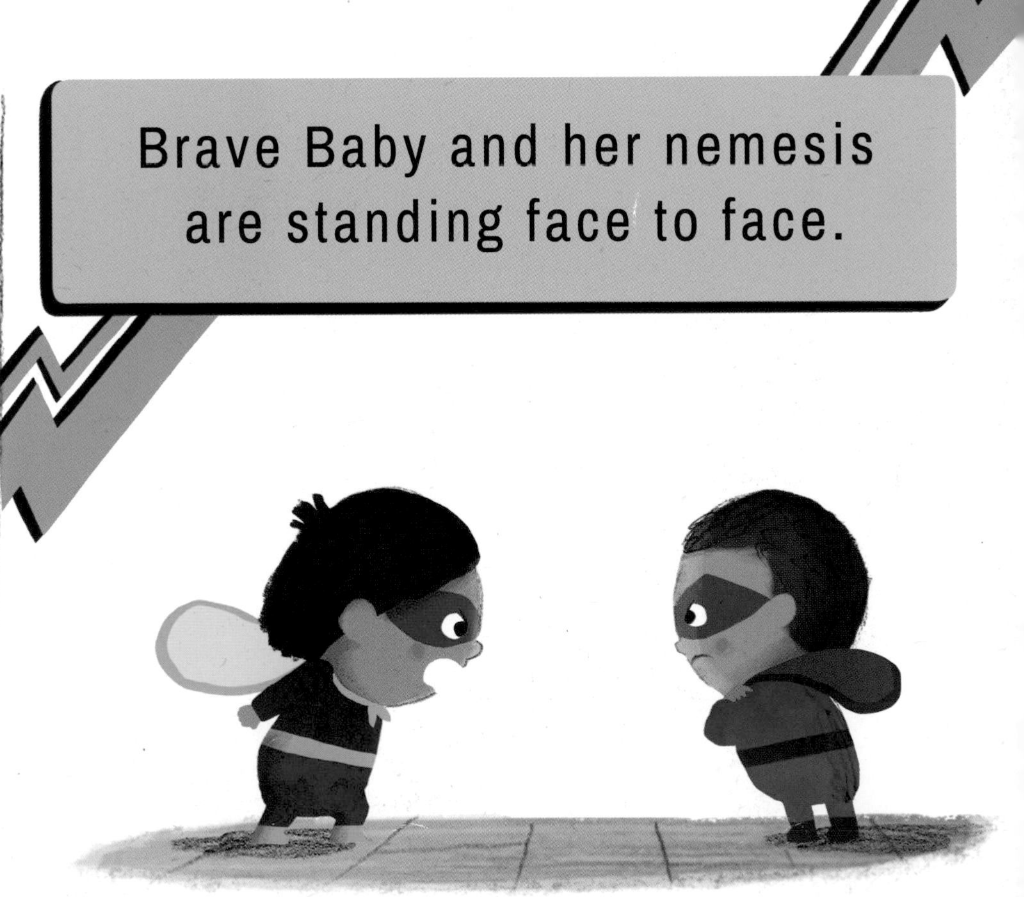

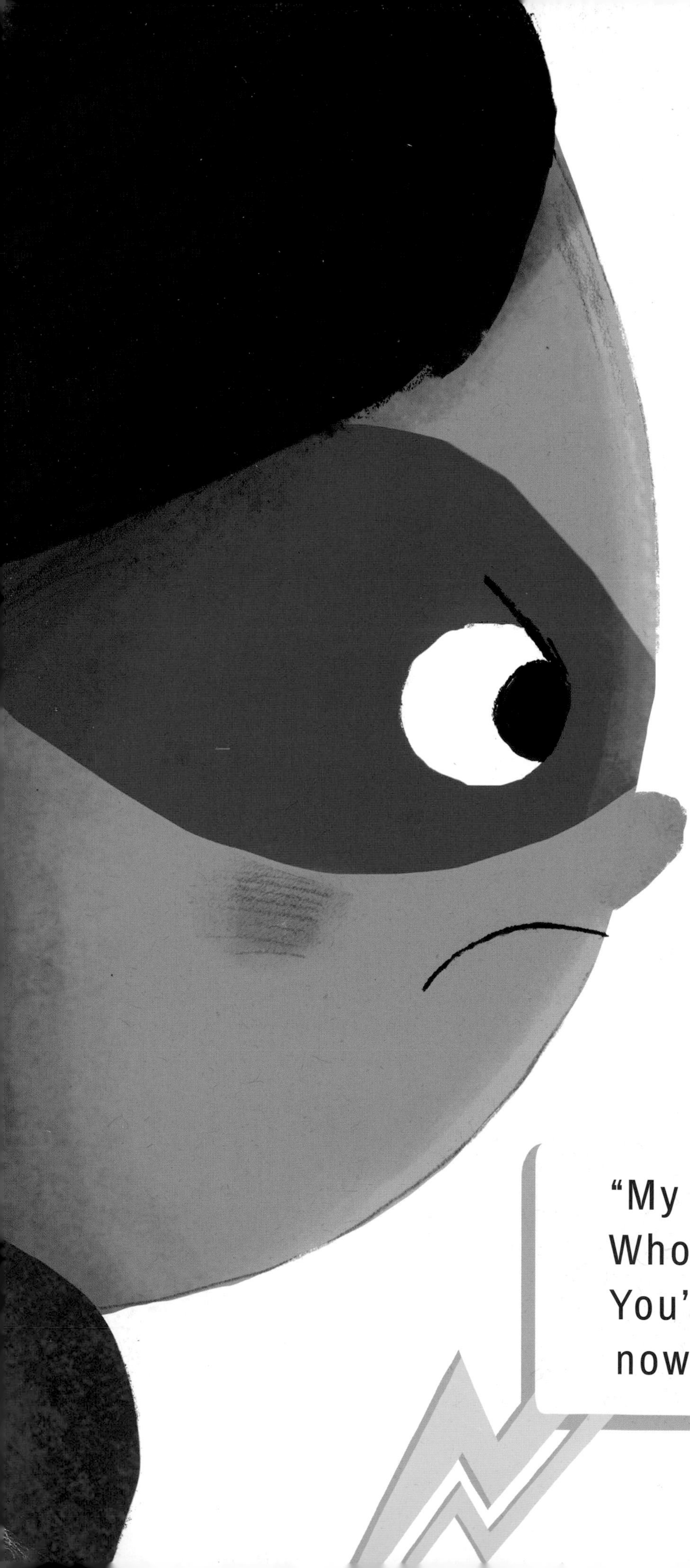

"My goody-two-shoes brother!
Whoever would have thought?
You're not so perfect after all,
now that you've been caught!

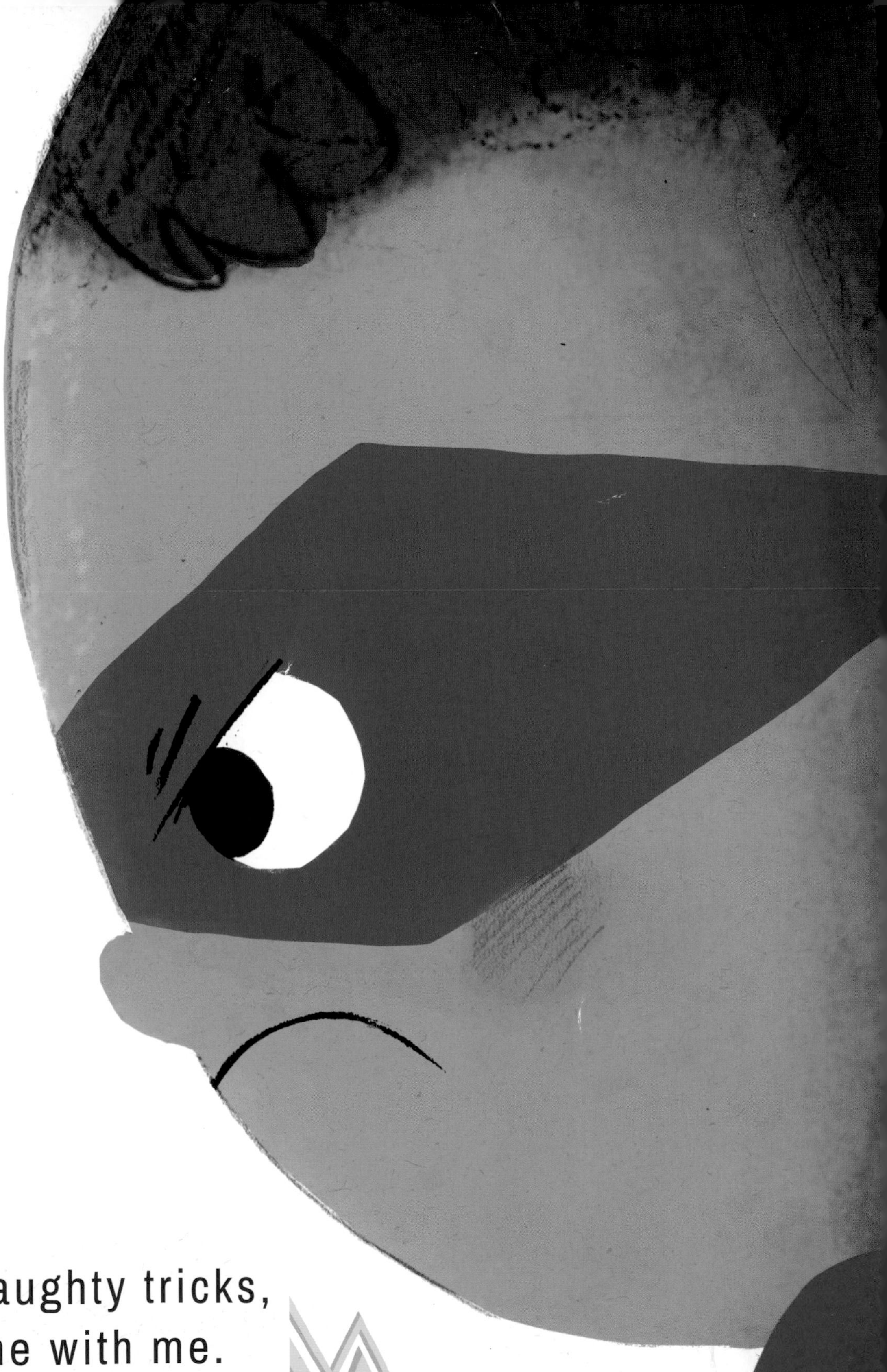

Enough of all your naughty tricks,
you're coming home with me.

Your days of crime are numbered,
just you wait and see!"

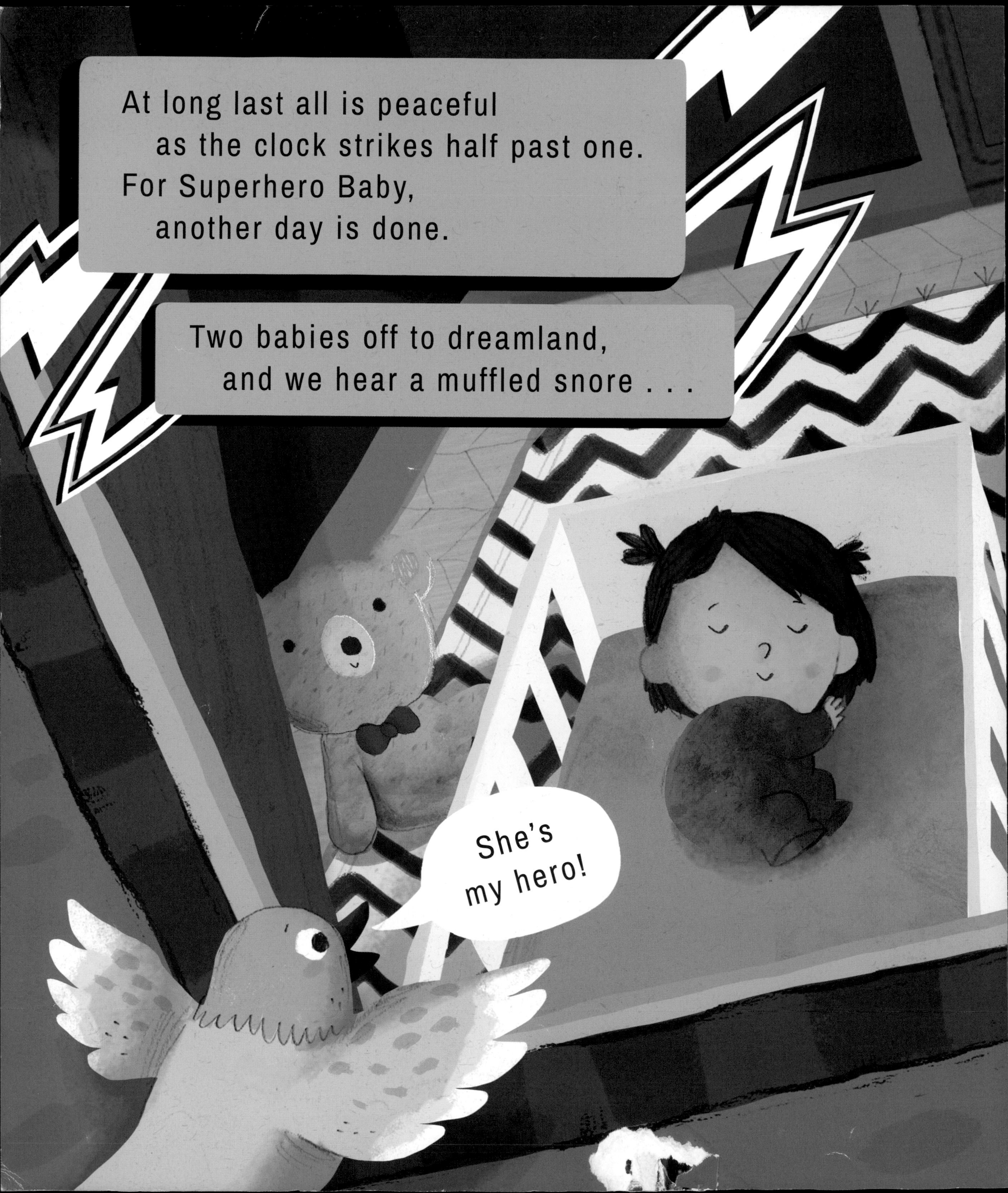
At long last all is peaceful
as the clock strikes half past one.
For Superhero Baby,
another day is done.
Two babies off to dreamland,
and we hear a muffled snore . . .
She's my hero!

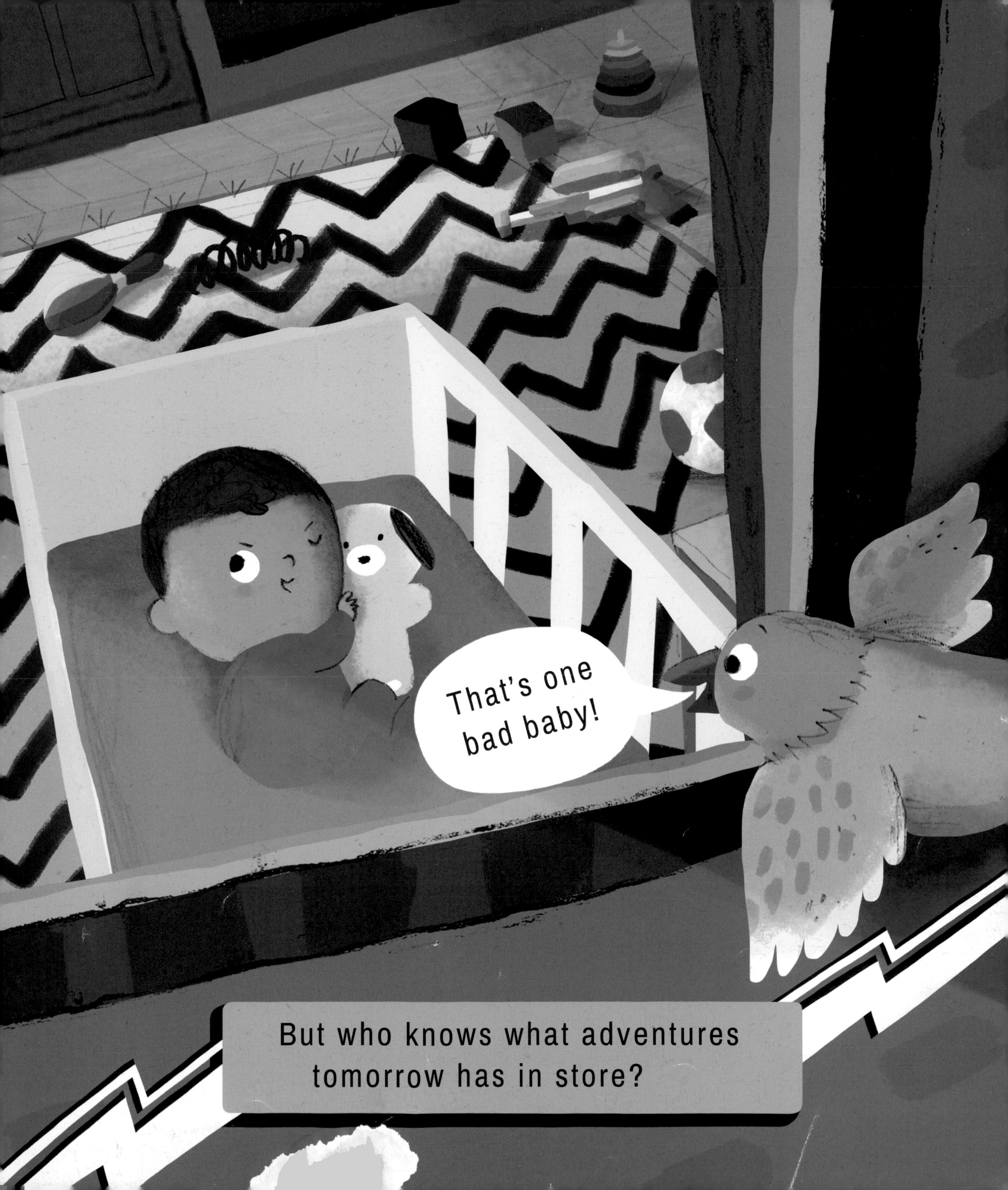
That's one bad baby!

But who knows what adventures tomorrow has in store?